MR. BUM
loses his memory

Original concept by Roger Hargreaves
Illustrated and written by Adam Hargreaves

MR. MEN   **LITTLE MISS**

MR. MEN™ LITTLE MISS™ © THOIP (a SANRIO company)

Mr. Bump loses his memory © 1998 THOIP (a Sanrio company)
Printed and published under licence from Price Stern Sloan, Inc., Los Angeles.
This edition published in 2017 by Dean, an imprint of Egmont UK Limited,
The Yellow Building, 1 Nicholas Road, London W11 4AN

ISBN 978 0 6035 7409 2
68473/1
Printed in Estonia

Mr Bump is the sort of person who is always having accidents.

Small accidents.

Medium-sized accidents.

And big accidents.

Lots and lots of accidents.

One day Mr Bump got out of bed, or rather, he fell out of bed as he did every morning.

He drew back the curtains and opened the window.

It was a beautiful day.

He leant on the window sill and breathed in deeply and ... fell out of the window.

BUMP!

Mr Bump sat up and rubbed his head. And as he rubbed, it dawned on him that he had no idea where he was.

He had no idea whose garden he was sitting in.

He had no idea whose house he was sitting in front of.

And he had no idea who he was.

Mr Bump had lost his memory.

Mr Bump walked up to his garden gate and looked down the lane.

Mr Muddle was passing by.

"Good afternoon," said Mr Muddle.

As you and I know, it was morning. But Mr Muddle, not surprisingly, always gets things in a muddle.

"I seem to have lost my memory," said Mr Bump. "Do you know what my name is?"

"You're Mr Careful," said Mr Muddle.

"Thank you," said Mr Bump.

Mr Bump went into town.

The first person he met was Mrs Packet the grocer, carrying an armful of groceries.

"Hello," said Mr Bump, "I'm Mr Careful, can I help?"

"Just the person! I need someone careful to deliver these eggs."

Mr Bump took the eggs from Mrs Packet and set off down the high street.

And because he was Mr Bump he slipped and fell on the eggs, breaking all of them.

"You're not all that careful, are you?" said Mrs Packet.

"Sorry," said Mr Bump.

He walked on past the dairy. Mr Bottle the manager came out.

"I'm looking for someone to drive the milk float," he said. "What's your name?"

"Mr Careful," replied Mr Bump.

"Perfect," said Mr Bottle. "I need someone careful to do the milk round."

Mr Bump set off down the road.

As he rounded the corner he hit the curb and the milk float turned over, smashing all the milk bottles.

"Well, that wasn't very carefully done, was it?" said Mr Bottle.

"Sorry," said Mr Bump.

Then he met Mr Brush the painter, who was up a ladder, painting.

"Hello," said Mr Bump. "I'm Mr Careful. Do you need a hand?"

"Yes please," replied Mr Brush. "I need someone careful to pass me that paint pot."

Mr Bump began to climb the ladder.

And being Mr Bump he fell off and the pot of paint landed on his head.

Mr Bump went for a walk.

"I don't understand it," he said to himself. "My name is Mr Careful, but I can't do anything carefully!"

It was then that he walked into a tree.

BUMP!

And bumped his head.

An apple fell out of the tree into his hand.

"That's odd," he said to himself. "How did I get here? The last thing I remember is opening my bedroom window."

" ... And where did all this paint come from?"

You know, don't you?

Just at that moment Farmer Fields turned up.

"Careful ... " he called.

"That sounds familiar," said Mr Bump, and fell down the bank into the river.